A Molly The Cat Book

BREWSTER

By Joseph S. Bonsall

Illustrated by Erin Marie Mauterer

Ideals Children's Books • Nashville, Tennessee
an imprint of Hambleton-Hill Publishing, Inc.

Text copyright © 1999 by Joseph S. Bonsall
Illustrations copyright © 1999 by Hambleton-Hill Publishing, Inc.

Published by Ideals Children's Books
An imprint of Hambleton-Hill Publishing, Inc.
1501 County Hospital Road
Nashville, Tennessee 37218

Printed and bound in the United States of America
ISBN 1-57102-149-3

Library of Congress Cataloging-in-Publication Data
Bonsall, Joseph S.
Brewster / written by Joseph S. Bonsall; illustrated by Erin Marie Mauterer.
p.   cm. (A Molly the cat book)
Summary: Brewster the bulldog saves Molly the cat from disaster.
ISBN 1-57102-149-3 (hardcover)
[1. Dogs—Fiction. 2. Cats—Fiction.] I. Mauterer, Erin, ill. II. Title. III.
Series: Bonsall, Joseph. Molly the cat book.
PZ7.B64273Br   1999
[Fic]—dc21   98-48019
                                                              CIP
                                                                  AC

Visit Molly and her friends on the World Wide Web at
www.mollythecat.com

Be not forgetful to entertain strangers:
for thereby some have entertained angels unawares.

— Hebrews 13:2

Molly was stretched out on the windowsill, warming herself in the afternoon sun and thinking about Outside. Molly loved the Outside, even though wise old Pumpkin, Omaha, and Gypsy always advised her against ever going there. Molly and her friends were indoor kitties who lived at the Home with Mother Mary, the wonderful humancat who loved them and took care of them. A loud, male humancat named Honey also lived in the Home. All the kitties liked it best when Honey was away on a trip!

It had been a long time since Molly's last adventure and she wanted to go Outside again. She couldn't stop thinking about it.

Molly ran downstairs to find her friend Omaha. He was playing on the floor with Molly's rainbow pillow. Pumpkin and Gypsy were asleep on the couch.

"I have something to tell you," said Molly, and she shared her plans with Omaha.

"You can't go Outside again, Molly. You just can't!" cried Omaha.

"Oh, you worry too much," meowed Molly in perfect catspeak. "Besides, it is so much fun out there."

"Have you forgotten that mean red cat? If it wasn't for Spooker and The Dude, he would have eaten you."

"I don't care. My mind is made up. Now, don't say anything to Pumpkin or Gypsy; they sleep all day anyway. I'll be home before anyone realizes that I'm gone."

Omaha started to cry.

"I'll be okay, Omi, I promise," Molly purred. "I won't go very far and I'll be back before you know it!"

Molly took off, slipping out the front door when Honey went to get the morning paper. She ran down the hill and into the woods.

Back at the Home, Omaha bowed his head and prayed to the God of All Creatures. "If it is not too much to ask, would you please look after Molly again and bring her safely home? She is so hard headed."

Molly weaved a path through the flowers and fields and meowed with delight at all of the beautiful sounds and smells of the Outside world.

Suddenly, Molly sensed danger. She stood still and held her breath. Afraid that a potential enemy might sense her fear and find her, Molly took off running!

"Grrrrr! Woof, woooooofffff!" A big yellow dog was running after her! Molly ran hard through the woods until she came upon a big road. Just as she started to run across, she heard a loud, awful noise, and then everything went dark.

When Molly woke up, she didn't know where she was. She tried to get up, but her legs and back hurt.

Where am I? she thought. *What happened? Why does it hurt me to move?*

"You are going to be fine, little one," whispered a gentle voice. "You just need to rest. You were hurt when you ran into a car. We are looking after you now."

"But, how did I get here? Where is here?" Molly asked.

"Brewster brought you. This is where he lives," the voice replied. "We have been taking care of you for days now and it is an answer to our prayers that you are getting better." Then the familiar-sounding voice was gone.

Molly tried to clear her head. Had she really been gone from the Home for days? *Everyone there must be so worried*, she thought.

Molly opened her eyes and looked around. She could tell that it was morning because she could see sunlight shining through the opening between two low boards.

Molly also smelled DOG!

"Arrggghh! Woof!" Something was waking up in the corner! "Oowwooff!"

Molly suddenly found herself face-to-face with the most hideous-looking creature that she had ever seen!

Now this wasn't just a dog. It was a bulldog! Molly had seen a lot of dogs go by the Home. However, this slobbering, roundish creature with his squashed nose and pushed in face beat just about all that the little calico had ever seen.

"Uuuuhhhhhmmm!" the dog yawned. His huge mouth opened so wide that Molly could see his big teeth. The dog drooled a little down the front of his leg, then slowly began to stretch.

Molly was shaking but remembered the advice of old Pumpkin: "Now, dogs are dangerous, but they are dumber than kitty litter. If one ever has you in a corner, do not show fear! Just take off running. There isn't a dog in the world that can catch a kitty with a good start!"

Well, Molly thought, *I tried that once and look where it got me!* Gypsy's advice seemed better: "Just hiss and spit and come out scratching!"

Molly hissed and spit!

"Wh...wh...whhhhaaatttt? Wooooof!" exclaimed the dog in total surprise. He turned and thump! ran right into the wall. Molly laughed out loud.

The strange dog shook his head from side to side so fast that his eyes rolled back in his head and spit flew everywhere.

"That is so gross!" Molly squealed at the dog, almost forgetting how very scared she had been only moments before.

"Wooofff," said the dog, "you're awake now. Are you, uh, ok?"

Molly was shocked. She could actually understand DOG!

"Are you Brewster?" she asked.

"Uhhh, yes, I am. Yes, yes, I'm Brewster, for sure I am! How did you know?"

"Well, there was someone else here a little while ago, a female cat, I think. She was so sweet. She told me that Brewster lived here. Do you mean to harm me?" she asked.

"Oh, no, no, no," answered the dog. "I wouldn't hurt you, little kitty. Uh, I was only having fun when I chased you!"

"What!" cried Molly, her fur rising up. "You're the dog that chased me?"

"OOPS! Now don't get m-mad at me, little kitty. I chased you, but I didn't mean for you to get hurt. That is why I brought you to my home. No one else is around here except my old master, Ben, who lives across the way. He's taken care of me since I was a puppy. He doesn't like cats but he never walks back here, anyway."

"Brewster?" asked Molly. "Do you know where my home is? Could you take me there?"

"Uh, I really don't know where anything is. Woooof!" Brewster replied.

Somehow, that doesn't surprise me, thought Molly.

"I'm going to find us some food," barked Brewster as he headed for the opening in the tool shed.

Over by the Home, Spooker and The Dude had been goofing off when they heard a yowl from Gypsy. Once again, she told them, Molly had run off and the mood at the Home was mighty grim. Spooker swore to Omaha, Pumpkin, and Gypsy that he and The Dude would once again find the little calico.

Spooker and The Dude were quite a sight. The battered looking old white cat and the handsome, black, Persian-type kitty walked side by side, searching the woods and fields for little Molly.

"Dude, we just have to find Molly," said Spooker. "Everyone loves her so much."

"Well, girls just want to have fun, you know," replied The Dude. "She is a little foolish, however. The God of All Creatures really does watch over that little girl! Molly will be fine. I just know it!"

Back in Brewster's shed, Molly was feeling much better. She felt the strength in her legs and her back returning. *Thank the God of All Creatures*, she thought.

Just then Brewster appeared, dragging a bag of smelly garbage. "Dinnertime," he barked.

"Yuk, what IS that?" asked Molly.

"Just some food that my master, Ben, didn't eat, so I brought it to you," woofed Brewster.

This is really disgusting, thought Molly. Then she remembered that outdoor kitties usually had to eat whatever they could get, and besides, she was starving, so Molly and Brewster dined on old Ben's leftovers.

Soon afterward, Brewster fell asleep and was slobbering and snoring at the same time. Molly, thinking he must be having goofy dog dreams, could not help but laugh at the sounds he made. *If there were a dog at the Home, I really do not think I could take it*, she thought.

Although Molly was grateful to Brewster for looking after her, she decided it was time to leave. She walked over to him and kissed him softly on the forehead, then slipped out just before the sun came up. She passed old Ben's house, then carefully crossed the road and disappeared into the trees.

Molly's old enemy, Red, was searching for some breakfast when he spied Molly walking through the trees. He immediately jumped out of the weeds and pounced on top of her, biting and clawing. Even though her back still hurt, Molly managed to summon enough strength to push the big cat away from her.

Red's ears were straight back, his fur on edge, and a low growl came from deep in his throat. "I told you I would get you!" he hissed in broken catspeak.

Molly took a step back. "You really do have a problem," she meowed tearfully.

Meanwhile, back at the toolshed, a voice was saying, "Brewster, wake up. Wake up!"

"Wh-a-a-t?" the bulldog answered sleepily.

"Molly is in trouble!"

"Woof! Who is there?" asked the bulldog as his eyes popped open.

"I am Angel. Now move it! You will know the way!"

Brewster was suddenly wide awake, his heart filled with concern for Molly. He ran through the opening, bolted past his master's house and crossed the road, moving as fast as he could.

He saw the big red cat poised to attack Molly. He caught the cat in his wide mouth and in one motion sent him hurtling through the air! Red landed with a crashing thud as the big dog ran over and sat down on top of him.

Red groaned and tried to move. "Ooooooowwwwww," he groaned.

Brewster turned his head and looked the mean cat right in the eye. "If you ever try to hurt my friend Molly again, I will bite your head clean off!" exclaimed Brewster.

Molly giggled as the bulldog slobbered all over Red. "Thanks, Brewster," she purred.

"You really need to thank Angel! Woooooofff!"

"Angel?" asked Molly.

Brewster tried to explain about the strange sweet voice that woke him and sent him to save Molly. It reminded Molly of the comforting voice that often spoke to her, but she had always believed that it was just a dream.

"So, how are you going to find your way home, little kitty?" said the bulldog, interrupting Molly's thoughts. "You can stay with me. Wooof! I would protect you."

"I know you would, Brewster. It's just that I have to go home now," Molly explained. "I really miss my friends and Mother Mary."

Suddenly Molly heard a familiar voice that made her squeal with delight.

"Hi there, Molly! Want to go home?" meowed Spooker with a grin.

"Help!" yelled Red. "Make him get off of me!"

"Catch the short end of the stick again, Red boy, or did you just fall over a cliff?" laughed The Dude.

"You better let him up now, Brewster," laughed Molly. Brewster removed himself from the now flattened enemy.

"Thanks for nothing. I almost drowned in dog drool," snarled the mean red cat as he streaked away.

"Thanks for taking care of Molly," Spooker said to Brewster. "We'll look after her now. I promised her friends I'd bring her back."

Molly was so happy to be going home that she was in tears. She turned to the bulldog and saw that he was crying, too.

"Good-bye, little Molly. I'm going to miss you. I wish I could take you home, but I have to stay with my master. I'm all he has."

Molly realized how very lucky she was to have so many friends who cared about her. So many creatures seemed to be alone.

"Good-bye, good friend," said Molly. "I can never thank you enough for all that you have done for me. I love you."

"Wooooof," barked the bulldog as he disappeared into the brush.

"That Brewster is a strange one," said the old white cat as the three kitties started toward the Home.

"Well, he IS a dog!" laughed Molly. "I will never forget him though. He saved my life. I love him very much."

"He is also the ugliest creature that I have ever seen in my life," added Spooker.

Molly jumped on Spooker's head and they wrestled playfully.

"Well, I'm going home now," meowed The Dude. "Spooker can see you the rest of the way, Molly. These old bones are tired."

"Good-bye, Dude. Thanks for all you have done for me!" said Molly.

"I'll see you around, old friend!" yelled Spooker as they walked on. "You take care!"

Spooker and Molly walked in silence for a long time. Then they stopped to rest beneath an old oak tree overlooking a beautiful valley. The Home was just a little farther over the next hill.

"Molly, do you remember the day we met?" asked Spooker.

"Yes, I do."

"Well, the reason I first came to the Home was because I had a story to tell you."

"I remember. You said we had to talk someday," whispered Molly.

"Molly," said Spooker, sitting up tall. "I knew your mother."

Molly didn't know what to say. She was always dreaming of her wonderful mother who had saved her when she was just a very small kitten. There had been some mean humancats who might have harmed her, so Molly's mother took her away from them. The mother cat carried little Molly for miles in the pouring rain and finally placed her in the path of a young male humancat who had picked her up and carried her to the Home. Molly remembered that her mother had always prayed for her and that her voice sounded so soft and sweet.

"Tell me the story, Spooker," she pleaded.

"A year or so ago," the black cat began, "there was a big fire at the old farmhouse where your mother lived. There was a humancat child trapped inside. Your precious mother ran into the flames and, all by herself, pulled that little one out. The child lived, but your mother was hurt very badly. She ran into the woods and hid."

"We all loved her very much. She was so wonderful." Spooker began to cry, gathered himself a little, and went on. "I found her just before the God of all Creatures took her to the Better Place. She told me about you, Molly, and how much she loved you and how very special you were. I guess I thought the time was right and that you should know. She had a tough life, but she was so full of love. The first time I saw you I knew that you were Angel's little girl."

"Angel is my mom?" Molly cried with joy in her heart. "She is still watching over me, Spooker."

The two kitties wept with joy.

Spooker and Molly walked side by side, down into the valley and over the hill towards the Home, where Pumpkin, Gypsy, Omaha, Mother Mary, and Honey would be waiting. A wondrous light seemed to shine all around them. Angel was watching.